MUCH ADO ABOUT ALDO

Aldo's older sister laughs when he refers to the family cats as his brothers, so he is triumphant when his teacher announces a project on the relationship of man and animals. When crickets arrive in the classroom to inhabit carefully prepared terrariums, naming the creatures and observing them makes school even more interesting than usual. Then, however, a package of chameleons also arrives, and Aldo realizes that the relationship they are studying is that between the consumer and the consumed. Profoundly shocked, Aldo gives up eating meat and embarks on a desperate attempt to save the crickets.

"The author has a remarkable ability to project the amusements and worries of childhood, conveying them in a deceptively simple style."

—*Horn Book*

BOOKS BY JOHANNA HURWITZ

Much Ado About Aldo
Aldo Applesauce
Aldo Ice Cream
Rip-Roaring Russell
Russell Rides Again
Russell Sprouts
The Rabbi's Girls

Johanna Hurwitz

MUCH ADO
ABOUT ALDO

pictures by John Wallner

A TRUMPET CLUB SPECIAL EDITION

Published by The Trumpet Club
666 Fifth Avenue, New York, New York 10103

Copyright © Johanna Hurwitz, 1978

ISBN: 0-440-84383-9

This edition published by arrangement with Viking Penguin,
a division of Penguin Books USA Inc.
Set in Baskerville
Printed in the United States of America
November 1990

10 9 8 7 6 5 4 3 2 1
OPM

For my nieces and nephews,
real and honorary:
Teddy and Daniel Frank
Sebastian, Garance, and Vanessa Ruta
Jeffrey and Nina Webb

Contents

1

Introducing Aldo

Aldo Sossi was starving. Every day when he came home from school his stomach felt as if he hadn't eaten a thing for weeks. Of course this wasn't true. Aldo had eaten lunch at noon with the rest of the third grade. But, by three o'clock, he could hardly remember it. His tuna-fish or salami sandwich seemed like a memory from years gone by.

So the first thing Aldo always did when he entered his family's apartment was to drop his books in his bedroom and to run to the kitchen for a snack.

Maybe there would be a drumstick left from last night's chicken dinner. Opening the refrigerator, Aldo saw that he was in luck. He took the chicken leg and sat down with it at the kitchen table. Immediately he had company. Peabody and Poughkeepsie, the two male cats who were part of the Sossi household, were never far away when someone was eating, especially if they were eating chicken.

Aldo was hungry. But he loved the cats as if they were his brothers. In fact, he thought of them as if they *were* his brothers. Originally the two kittens had been gifts to Aldo's big sisters, Elaine and Karen. That was nine years ago before Aldo, who was only eight, was even born. Now Elaine was thirteen and Karen was eleven and a half, and they both tended to ignore the cats. Aldo was the one who fed them and cleaned out the litter pan. And Aldo was the one who played games with them, rolling balls down the apartment hallway for them to chase or pulling a long piece of string for them to try and catch.

So now, with both cats rubbing against his ankles, Aldo could not resist. Even though he was starving, he pulled off a piece of chicken and broke it in two. He tossed the scraps onto the kitchen floor, and the cats pounced upon them. They seemed to swallow the bits whole, because at once they were ready for more. But Aldo had finished the drumstick, and there was nothing more to share. He took it and carefully placed it in the garbage pail. The cats would have loved chewing on the bone, but chicken bones were dangerous for cats, and Aldo didn't want them to get hurt. So even though Peabody meowed loudly in protest, Aldo fastened the pail firmly shut. At such moments Aldo could understand why his mother made him wear his raincoat to school on cloudy days. He didn't like wearing his raincoat, especially since most of the time it didn't rain. But Mrs. Sossi felt it was her responsibility to make Aldo wear it, just as Aldo felt it was his responsibility to protect the cats from chicken bones.

Aldo heard voices at the door and the lock opening. Elaine and Karen were coming home from junior high school.

"Where's Mom?" asked Karen, walking into the kitchen.

Aldo pointed to the note on the table. It was from their mother and said that she had gone shopping and probably wouldn't be home until after four o'clock.

"What happened in school today?" Aldo asked his sisters. He liked to hear about what went on in the upper grades so he would be prepared when he got there. Unfortunately, neither sister discussed her classes very much.

Elaine poured herself a glass of milk.

"Do you want to hear what I did in school?" asked Aldo. He loved to report on what he did.

"No, thanks," said Elaine with a bored expression. "I've already been through third grade once."

Aldo sighed, but he was not discouraged. His mother was a good listener, and it was almost four o'clock. Still, he made another attempt at conversation.

"At school Jeffrey told me that he heard on TV that a year in a cat's life is equal to seven years in a human life. That means that Peabody and Poughkeepsie are older than Mom and Dad. Seven times nine is sixty-three. That's the same age as Grandpa. Isn't that interesting?" asked Aldo.

"Very interesting," said Elaine, sounding as bored as ever. At thirteen she had her own interests: boys. A younger brother didn't count. "Maybe by the time I'm sixty-three, Mom will finally let me get my ears pierced," she said. Piercing her ears was a new obsession with her, and she had a running argument about it with her parents.

Karen didn't want to have her ears pierced. She was sure it would hurt too much. Karen's prime interest these days was the telephone book. She didn't phone anyone, but she read the enormous Manhattan directory with great absorption. She was keeping a list of famous names that she found. There were eleven listings for CARTER, JAMES and two for CARTER, AMY. Karen knew that none of them represented the real President Carter and his daughter, but she enjoyed making her lists, nevertheless. Among the other names that she had found were WEBB, CHARLOTTE and MOORE, MARY T. She insisted that the *T* stood for Tyler. Karen kept a notebook in which she wrote down all her famous names.

When Aldo looked in the telephone book, he always turned to *S* and looked for his father's listing, SOSSI, GEORGE. Someday he would have a telephone and his name would appear too. Seeing it there would be similar to seeing his name in the encyclopedia for some famous invention or discovery.

Sometimes Aldo tried to help Karen. Last week he had turned to pages with the letter *C*. Unfortunately, there was no one named COLUMBUS, CHRISTOPHER living in Manhattan. Or if he did live in the city, he didn't have a telephone. It was interesting to think about.

Now Aldo went to wash the chicken from his fingers. He thought he would play with Peabody and Poughkeepsie for a little while before he did his homework. He had gotten three words wrong on the spelling test this morning, and he had to write each word five times. One of the words had been *chicken*. Another misspelled word was *potato*.

Even with the chicken leg inside him, as he dried his hands and thought about his spelling homework, Aldo couldn't help wondering what they would have that night for supper.

2

Aldo at School

At school Aldo Sossi was not the smartest boy in the third grade. Neither was he the best athlete nor the loudest nor the tallest nor the shortest. In short, at first glance he did not stand out in a crowd. Yet when the third-grade teachers met with Mr. Howard, the principal of P.S. 35, to discuss their students, Aldo's teacher, Mrs. Dowling, called him the most interested student she had taught in many years.

"You mean the most interesting?" asked Mr. Howard.

"No," said Mrs. Dowling. "Aldo is the most *interested*. He is interested in everything."

And it was true. Aldo was interested in spelling and why words were made up of the odd combinations of letters. He couldn't understand why a word like *one* was spelled that way. And he knew what he meant when he wrote *chiken* on the paper. After he learned about the extra *c* he remembered it. But the problem was that the following week he made another mistake. This time he wrote *chickon*. So his spelling tests came back with lots of red *x*'s. But the corrections weren't because he had no interest. Aldo had as much interest in spelling as Bruce, who always won the marshmallow that Mrs. Dowling awarded for a perfect spelling paper.

Aldo was interested in arithmetic. He actually *liked* the times tables. It was interesting to him that 4 times 12 was the same as 6 times 8, or that 5 times 8 was the same as 4 times 10.

During social studies Aldo asked the most questions. He was never bored with the filmstrips about life in other climates. When Mrs. Dowling was out sick and the class had a substitute teacher, Aldo was the one who remembered what page they were up to in their workbooks and what they had been talking about the day before.

Aldo was interested in playing the recorder with his classmates in music. He played many wrong notes and his melodies were hard to recognize, but Aldo was interested in music.

Yet of all the school subjects, there was one that interested Aldo most. It was science, especially learning about animals.

When he was little, Aldo had loved to look at pictures of dinosaurs in the encyclopedia. At a very young age he was able to distinguish a Brontosaurus from a Brachiosaurus and a Stegosaurus from a Styracosaurus. He had loved saying those long, important-sounding names to himself over and over again. But as Aldo got older, he became less interested in prehistoric animals and more interested in the real animals around him. That was why he loved his cats so much. He liked to peek into the pink inside of their ears or study their mouths when they yawned. Even when they were sleeping he found them interesting. He wondered if cats had dreams and decided that they did, because often Peabody or Poughkeepsie would twitch or move in his sleep as if reacting to something.

Aldo wished that his family included a dog also, but he realized that he was lucky to have two cats. City apartments were not convenient places for pets, and most of his friends had neither a cat nor a dog.

One of Aldo's friends, Jerry, had a turtle, and Aldo enjoyed watching him too. All the other third graders thought the zoo was a place to take babies. But secretly Aldo still loved going there and studying the animals and how they acted. He loved the sea lions gliding in and out of the water, and he was fascinated by the huge wrinkled elephants. Most of all he liked the monkey house with all the varieties of apes and chimpanzees. Aldo could stand and watch them all day long. They looked just like people.

So when Mrs. Dowling announced to the third graders that in a few weeks they were go-

ing to study the relationship between man and animals, Aldo became very interested. Third grade got more interesting every day.

Aldo remembered that Elaine had once heard him referring to Peabody and Poughkeepsie as his brothers and she had teased him dreadfully.

"Stupid! You can't be related to a cat!" she taunted. Yet here was Mrs. Dowling, who was a teacher so she ought to know, saying that there was an important relationship between man and animals.

"We would not be able to exist without them," said Mrs. Dowling.

Aldo could not wait to get home and see his brothers and to tell Elaine what Mrs. Dowling had said.

3

Peabody in a Pickle

One Friday, about a week later, Aldo came home from school and was greeted by the smell of fresh paint. It was a nice odor and he liked it.

"What are you doing?" he asked his mother, though it was quite obvious what she was doing.

"I've just repainted Karen's chest of drawers and Elaine's desk for their new room," she said.

"Can I help?" begged Aldo.

"I'm all done," his mother said. "I started early so the furniture would have plenty of time to dry. I want the girls to finish fixing up their new room over the weekend."

The girls' new room was their parents' old room. They had just switched to give the girls more space. Aldo went to his room to drop his jacket and school books on his bed. He was the only one in the family to have a private room. Even the cats shared a single basket, though they hardly ever chose to sleep in it.

Aldo's room was very tiny. Some people probably had closets bigger than his room. The room had been designed for a maid seventy-five years ago when the apartment building had been planned and many people had live-in household help.

One of the cats was sleeping on Aldo's bed. Although they were brothers, born in the same litter, they were not twins and they were easy to tell apart. They both were black and white. Peabody's black was specked with white in a way that everyone said was quite unusual. The specks were small, hardly bigger than peas, which was how he got his name. He was the adventurer, the first to climb into the box in which the groceries had been delivered and the first to look for mischief. (He knew how to open doors and garbage pails). Poughkeepsie had a white spot on his head and two white legs. He studied all situations and walked about the apartment with silent dignity more befitting a creature whose age was equivalent to sixty-three years. The cat on the bed was obviously Poughkeepsie.

Aldo put his books down gently, but his movements woke the cat. Poughkeepsie yawned and stretched out his front legs in a very human gesture.

"Hi, Pouks!" Aldo said, calling the cat by his private nickname. "Where's Peabody?"

There was no response from Poughkeepsie, and Aldo had not expected one. He went into the kitchen for a snack, and the cat followed him.

Aldo took an apple and a handful of pretzels and went to see what was on TV. Before he sat down on the sofa, he looked under it in case Peabody was there. He wasn't, so Aldo turned his attention to the afternoon cartoons.

Elaine and Karen came home from their school and admired their newly painted furniture. The next thing Aldo knew, his mother was calling him to supper.

They had chicken for supper again that night. Poughkeepsie came and as usual rubbed against the legs of each person in turn, hoping for a little tidbit.

"Hey. Where's Peabody?" asked Aldo.

Peabody was conspicuously missing. During chicken dinners he always meowed loudly, reminding everyone that he wanted a share of the meal too.

"He must be off sleeping," said Aldo's father, laughing. "He knows that we'll put something aside for him."

"His old age, that Aldo keeps talking about, is finally catching up with him," said Elaine.

"What happened in school today?" Mr. Sossi asked his children, changing the subject.

Both Elaine and Karen shrugged their shoulders.

"Same old things," said Karen. "I'm glad tomorrow is Saturday."

"We planted grass," said Aldo.

"Grass? In this weather?" asked Mrs. Sossi. "Where did you plant it?"

Aldo put down the chicken wing that he was holding so he could explain better. "Mrs. Dowling has some old fish tanks, but there aren't any fish in them. So we put dirt in them, and then we planted grass seed. It was fun."

"Some fun!" said Elaine. "Where will you get a lawn mower small enough to cut the grass with?" she asked.

Aldo was used to his sister's sarcasm. "It's very interesting," he insisted, picking up his chicken wing again and taking a big bite.

After supper, Aldo washed the cats' dishes and put out fresh food for them. There were three dishes: one with moist food from a can, another with pellets of dry food, and a third dish with fresh water. Aldo put some scraps of chicken that his mother gave him in the dish with the canned food.

Peabody was so clever that usually just the sound of the opening of the kitchen drawer that held the can opener brought him running. Poughkeepsie waited patiently as Aldo set out the food. But there was still no sign of Peabody. Aldo listened as Poughkeepsie chewed on one of his hard pellets. The crunching noise always sounded delicious, like chewing on hard candies or cookies. Once Aldo had tasted a couple of the pellets. They were like hard, slightly fishy crackers and not very good. But then he wasn't a cat.

Aldo was bothered now that Peabody still wasn't about, so he set off on a systematic search. He looked in all of the cats' favorite corners: behind the living-room drapes, under all the beds, inside the laundry hamper, and on top of the radiators. Maybe he is lying dead somewhere, Aldo worried.

He called to Karen and Elaine, who were

busily arranging their possessions in their new room.

"This shelf is mine," Elaine said, pointing to the top one in the case. "Don't touch it!"

"Well, don't you touch this one," said Karen, with her hand on the shelf below Elaine's.

"Have you seen Peabody?" Aldo asked. "I haven't seen him once since I came home from school."

Neither of the girls had seen him either. They started looking too.

"Maybe he's in a closet," suggested Elaine, opening the one in her new bedroom. Soon every closet in the apartment had been inspected, and still there was no sign of Peabody.

Mr. and Mrs. Sossi helped too.

Suddenly Mrs. Sossi thought of something. "You know," she said, "this afternoon I opened the windows and the apartment door to air out the smell of the paint. Peabody must have gone out."

"Out the window!" gasped Aldo.

31

The Sossis' windows were five stories above the street. "He may have fallen to the sidewalk and died." Aldo shuddered.

"Keep calm," said Mr. Sossi. "Cats are expert climbers." But he put on his jacket, and he had a worried expression on his face as he went to look outside on the street.

4

The Search

The thought of Peabody out roaming in the street was upsetting to all the Sossis. He and Poughkeepsie were house cats, which meant that they had never set foot on the street in all their lives. Except for an occasional trip inside the cat carrier to the veterinarian for shots, they had never been out-of-doors.

"If he went out the door instead of out the window, he could still be in the building somewhere," offered Mrs. Sossi.

Aldo liked that idea much better.

"Let's look for him in the halls," he said.

Karen and Elaine went with him. They decided to ride up to the top floor of the building in the elevator and then walk all the way down to search.

The top floor was the fifteenth. Peabody was not there. Nor was he on the fourteenth or twelfth, which were the next two floors down. There was no thirteenth floor because it was considered bad luck. Aldo wondered what could be worse luck than losing Peabody.

On the eleventh floor Karen said, "Maybe he's in someone's apartment. We should start ringing the doorbells and ask."

"There are too many," said Elaine. She almost always disagreed with whatever Karen said. Yet fourteen floors with ten apartments per floor meant one hundred and forty doorbells to ring. This time Elaine was right.

"I wish we had a loudspeaker like the school's," said Aldo, thinking of the public-address system the principal used to make announcements to the entire building at once.

"We could make a sign and hang it in the elevator," said Karen.

By now they had reached the eighth floor. "We could offer a reward—*Wanted Dead or Alive.*"

"No!" shouted Aldo. "He can't be dead."

They completed their search without success and took the elevator back to their apartment. Mr. Sossi had already returned without any good news either.

Elaine dug into the carton where her papers and markers were temporarily being stored while the paint on her desk dried. The two sisters bent over the paper, making the sign.

Lost
Black Cat With White Spots
Name—Peabody
Return to Apt. 5G—Sossi
Reward

"What will the reward be?" asked Aldo.

"I'll donate my big poster of Clark Gable that used to hang over my bed in my old room," offered Elaine. "I was thinking of getting a new poster anyhow."

"That's very big of you," said Mr. Sossi.

"Yes, it's a big poster too," said Elaine. "Let's add *Big* in front of *Reward* on the sign."

Mr. Sossi took the sign and a roll of tape and went to mount it in the elevator for everyone to see.

"Aldo! It's your bedtime," said his mother. "I bet by tomorrow morning someone will be at our door with Peabody."

Aldo had his own tiny bathroom, which was also supposed to be for the tiny nonexistent maid. As he stood brushing his teeth the door was pushed open and Poughkeepsie walked inside.

"Oh, Pouks," said Aldo, bending down and stroking the cat's soft fur. "I wish you could talk. I bet you know where Peabody went."

Just before he went to sleep, Aldo had an

38

idea. He took the box of hard cat pellets, and shaking it he walked through the apartment.

"Peabody! Peabody!" he called.

"Have you gone crazy?" asked Elaine. "He's not here. We already looked everywhere."

"I know." Aldo sighed. "I just thought in case he was asleep somewhere he would hear the food in the box and wake up."

"Nobody can hear anything with all this noise," shouted Mr. Sossi, for Elaine was playing her phonograph loudly.

"Aldo, go to sleep," his mother said gently. "Tomorrow's another day."

Aldo woke very early the next morning. He woke with an unhappy feeling, and for a moment he couldn't remember what was making him unhappy. Then it came to him. Peabody was missing.

He had been thinking about Peabody even in his sleep, imagining the cat calling to him. He got out of bed and began walking softly

40

about the apartment. Poughkeepsie was sleeping on the sofa, alone. Aldo looked at the still cat. Sometimes the two cat brothers slept so closely curled around one another that they looked like a single animal. The second look proved the first to have been correct. Poughkeepsie was alone.

Aldo thought he heard a meow. It was muffled, as if coming from very far away. He rushed to the door of the apartment, his heart beating quickly. As he turned the inside latch he heard the soft meow again. The door opened. There was no one and no cat there.

Aldo blinked away the tears of disappointment. He closed the door and again heard the faint meow of a cat. Peabody was around, or else it was his ghost.

There was another faint meow, and it sent Aldo rushing into his parents' room.

"Come help me. I hear Peabody, but I can't see him." He ran to his sisters' room, where the door had been left open all night because of the odor of fresh paint. "Wake up! Wake up! I hear Peabody."

Everyone listened. First there was silence, but after a few seconds the muffled cry of a cat was heard. Somehow it sounded both near and far-away at the same time. The family retraced their steps of the evening before about the apartment. From time to time the faint meow repeated itself, encouraging them to continue. No one could guess where it was coming from.

Aldo stood in the doorway of Elaine and Karen's new bedroom. He stood still for a moment, listening hard. He felt that the cat's cries were coming from this room. Yet he had looked in the closet and under the beds, and there was no sign of Peabody. The meow came once again. Suddenly Aldo darted across the room toward the newly painted desk. He pulled open first one and then another of the drawers. From the deep bottom drawer came another meow. There sat Peabody, looking about him sleepily. He let out a big yawn and jumped out of the drawer.

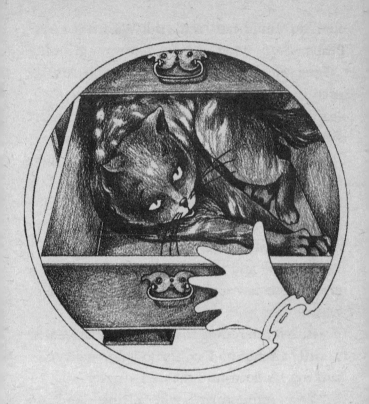

"You stupid cat!" said Aldo with love.

Mr. Sossi stood in the doorway, grinning. "Good work, Aldo. It looks as if you win the picture of Clark Gable."

"I don't want it," said Aldo. "I just wanted Peabody."

Elaine came into the room, smiling. "I guess I'll keep the poster after all," she said. "Ever since I saw *Gone with the Wind* on TV, I've liked it. I'm kind of used to having Clark in the room with me."

"I know," said Mrs. Sossi. "Just the way we're all used to having both Peabody and Poughkeepsie here with us."

"Isn't it interesting that a cat can survive with so little air and no food for so long," said Aldo, sticking his head into the desk drawer.

"Very interesting," said Elaine. And she didn't even sound bored.

5

The Class Project

The third grade had finished units on the desert, rain forests, mountains, and the plains. Some of the third graders complained that they were tired of studying about faraway places.

"There are no rain forests in New York City," said Jessica.

"And no deserts or mountains either," added Peter.

"The purpose of school," Mrs. Dowling reminded the class, "is to introduce you to all aspects of life. You already know about sidewalks. We are ready now to work on the new science unit that I told you about. It should interest everyone."

Aldo sat up straighter in his seat. This was what he had been waiting for.

"To begin with," Mrs. Dowling said, "today there will be an addition to our class."

"It better be another boy," called out Craig. At present there were three more girls in the class than boys, and most members of the minority were disturbed by this ratio.

"The new additions . . ." continued Mrs. Dowling dramatically.

"*Additions?*" Everyone chorused.

"Yes!" Mrs. Dowling smiled. "Male and female!" She lifted a small cardboard box from her desk.

"These are crickets, and they will live in the grasslands that we planted."

She walked to the back of the classroom toward the four terrariums, in which Aldo and his classmates had planted grass, clover, and mustard seed. Within days the seeds had sprouted.

46

It was funny to have grass growing indoors while there was still the slushy remains of the last snowfall outside.

The class gathered around Mrs. Dowling as she opened the box.

"Ugh! Bugs!" said Jessica, as Mrs. Dowling transferred the first of the insects into one of the tanks. Aldo noticed postage stamps on the box. The crickets had traveled to school by mail, just like a letter. Mrs. Dowling tipped the box into each of the terrariums in turn, and the small black insects moved into their new homes.

"Won't they climb out?" asked Aldo.

"Crickets don't climb, they jump," Mrs. Dowling informed the class.

Few of the students had ever seen a cricket before. They pushed one another to get a better view. Mrs. Dowling opened the bottom drawer of her desk and removed some plastic lids that had holes in them. She placed a lid over each tank. "Now the crickets won't be able to get out."

Then she told the students to return to their seats. Everyone was reluctant to leave these new pets.

Jeffrey was monitor for the week. Mrs. Dowling gave him sheets to distribute to the class. On each sheet was a large drawing of a cricket with all the parts of its body labeled.

Aldo figured that the crickets in the back of the room were mostly the size of his thumbnail. He placed his thumb on a corner of the drawing and tried to figure out how many crickets could fit on the giant drawing.

Mrs. Dowling explained to the class that the new unit would teach them about food chains and populations. "It shows the relationship of man and animals too. We will start with the crickets. They will eat the grass just as we eat certain plants," she said.

"Name one plant that you eat," she asked Peter.

He said corn, and she wrote the word on the blackboard. In a short while there was a long list of fruits and vegetables on the board. Aldo wondered why human beings didn't eat grass, and he made a secret resolve to try a piece in the park when it was spring.

Later in the morning, when he had completed his spelling assignment, Mrs. Dowling permitted Aldo to sit in the back of the room and watch the crickets.

"It's very interesting," he explained to her.

Most of the crickets lay still in the grass with just an occasional flicker of their antennae. They reminded Aldo of Peabody and Poughkeepsie and the way they could lie very still but would suddenly move their whiskers. Were the crickets sleeping? Aldo wondered. He was curious about whether the crickets could think. He wondered if they knew they were in New York. How would it feel to be a cricket in the grass out in the country somewhere, and then have someone put you in a box and mail you to a school?

Mrs. Dowling had said that though the crickets had wings, they couldn't fly with them. Yet if the box had come air mail, then these crickets had been given a chance to fly. The crickets were very interesting to think about. In fact, Aldo was so busy thinking that his stomach forgot to tell him it was time for lunch. He remembered only when the bell rang.

6

Crickets

During the next days whenever anyone completed their schoolwork, they were permitted to sit near the terrariums and observe the crickets.

Jennifer and Lisa started giving the crickets names. The first was Jiminy, which was the name given to the biggest and most active of the crickets. Then there was Licorice, and Blackie, and George and Martha Washington, and Bunny and Bugs. One tank held seven crickets named after the dwarfs who befriended Snow White.

"Can you really tell them apart?" asked Mrs. Dowling. Everyone insisted that it was possible.

Especially Aldo. He spent every moment that he could studying the crickets. He rushed through his classwork, misspelling words and adding and subtracting quickly and inaccurately so that he could watch the little black insects.

They were living creatures like Poughkeepsie and Peabody and just as fascinating. Aldo would open the lid of one of the terrariums and remove a cricket. He liked to hold it gently in his hand and feel the faint tickle as it walked across his palm.

Every day one student was permitted to open the lid of the tanks and sprinkle a little water on the grass and crickets.

When Jeffrey did, he said, "I'm making rain."

And Nina said, "It's not nice to fool Mother Nature." Yet the crickets appeared to be fooled and satisfied with their new life. Sometimes when it was very quiet in the classroom, like during silent-reading time, the children could hear them chirping.

"I guess the crickets enjoy being in third

grade," said Mrs. Sossi, when Aldo told her about them at home. Aldo was always telling his family about the crickets.

"I don't see what's so interesting about bugs," said Elaine. She was busy making a list of which of her friends already had their ears pierced. So far she had six names: Amy, Mara, Hilary, Celia, Katy, and Heather. She was sure there were some other girls in her class, but she couldn't remember.

Karen was sitting with the phone book in her lap. "Wouldn't it be funny if a person named Anne had the last name Cricket. She would be A. Cricket." Karen turned the pages hopefully. She found Cricket Sales Co. and Cricket Music Studios, but there was no Anne or Arthur or Andrew Cricket. She forgot about crickets and turned her attention to other possible C names.

Aldo turned to his mother. "Isn't it interesting that the crickets can have a whole little world inside the terrarium. It's like a tiny park for them. I could watch them all day long."

"Well, don't forget about your other school-work. Those spelling papers that I've been signing lately haven't been too good." Mrs. Dowling had a rule that every spelling paper had to be signed by a parent, even if the student got 100 percent.

"I do my work," said Aldo. "But crickets are the most interesting part of school."

"Erica!" shrieked Elaine.

"What's that?" asked Mrs. Sossi.

"I just thought of another name for my list," said Elaine, looking meaningfully at her mother.

"School certainly has changed since I was young," said Mrs. Sossi. "All you think about in junior high school is ears. And Aldo in the third grade thinks about bugs. What ever happened to arithmetic and history and geography and the other important subjects? And what about reading *real* books?" she asked, looking at Karen.

Elaine didn't bother to answer. She was working on her list. Karen was looking for a new name for her list too. But Aldo wasn't making any list, so he said, "Oh, Mom, you're only joking. You know we're learning lots of things. But crickets is the best subject I've ever learned at school."

7

Bad News
for the Crickets

Three weeks after the box of crickets was opened, a new box came addressed to Mrs. Dowling's class. It was larger and in it was a plastic bag filled with grass. Hiding in the grass were four chameleons, and each was quickly assigned to a tank.

For most of Aldo's classmates, the chameleons were an even more exciting addition to the class than the crickets. Ordinarily, Aldo would have been fascinated by these reptiles too.

They were as big as his longest finger and their tails made them three times longer still.

A cricket living with them might as well be living in the time of the dinosaurs. In fact, the chameleons reminded Aldo of a picture he had seen of Ornitholestes, which was a type of dinosaur. Aldo felt a chill run through his body.

Mrs. Dowling explained to the class about the chameleons. In nature these reptiles ate insects such as crickets. And that is exactly what they were going to do in the third-grade classroom.

Nobody else seemed to care, but to Aldo the idea seemed like murder.

"Nina? What did you have for dinner last night?" asked Mrs. Dowling.

"Fried chicken," Nina answered after a moment's thought.

Mrs. Dowling wrote the old spelling word *chicken* on the blackboard.

"Aldo, what did you have?"

"Hamburgers," Aldo answered.

"What animal do they come from?" she asked.

There was a pause while Aldo thought of the answer.

Bruce raised his hand and said, "Cows."

"That's right," Mrs. Dowling said. "Hamburger, steak, roast beef, and pot roast all come from cattle."

The word *cattle* was written on the board. The chalk squeaked, and Aldo gave another shiver. There was a bad taste in his mouth. He had never known a cow personally, but now that he thought about it eating cows and chickens was murder too.

"What other animals do we eat?" Mrs. Dowling asked. She added *pigs, ducks,* and *fish* to her list. Aldo stopped listening. He was thinking of Blackie and Licorice and Jiminy and all the other crickets closed in their tanks, waiting to be eaten by the chameleons. He left his seat and went out in the hall to the boys' washroom. He thought he might spit up his breakfast, because the feeling in his throat and mouth was so bad. Nothing happened and so after a few minutes he went back to the classroom.

The students were gathering their lunch

boxes and jackets in anticipation of the lunch bell. Aldo got his things, but he knew he wouldn't be able to eat. He had a liverwurst sandwich. He wasn't sure what sort of an animal a liverwurst was, and he wasn't even interested in finding out just now.

Lunch held no interest for him at all.

8

Bad News
for Mrs. Sossi

By the time Aldo returned home from school, he had regained his appetite enough to eat two bananas. But he was still thinking about the class discussion of food. He found Poughkeepsie and Peabody both curled up on the bed in his room. He sat on the floor by his bed watching them and thinking, "I'm glad nobody eats cats." And then he wondered how it was that both cats and dogs had succeeded in escaping the fate of almost all other animals. Birds, fish, insects were all eaten.

Aldo went to his sisters' room.

"You didn't knock!" said Elaine.

"Sorry," said Aldo. "Why do you suppose people eat so many animals?" he asked.

Elaine shrugged her shoulders. "They taste good," she said.

"But it's killing," said Aldo. "Every time people eat meat, animals have to be killed."

"Don't worry about it," said Karen. "They can't think so they don't know. You shouldn't think about it either." She pointed to the telephone directory. "Look what I just found." Her finger was under the name REDFORD, ROBERT.

"Good," said Aldo, but his heart wasn't in it. He was still thinking about eating animals. And he was thinking about the chameleons back at school and whether or not any of them had eaten any of the crickets yet.

That night at supper there were lamb chops. They didn't have them very often because of the high price. Aldo said he didn't want any.

"Are you feeling all right?" asked Mrs. Sossi. She reached across to feel Aldo's forehead.

66

"I'm fine," Aldo insisted. "I'm just not too hungry."

"Aldo doesn't want to eat animals," explained Karen.

Aldo did manage to eat a huge baked potato, carrots and peas, some salad, and he asked for a second piece of the cherry pie.

After supper Aldo took a sheet of paper and folded it in half. He made two lists:

YES	NO
peanut butter and grape jelly	liverwurst
peanut butter and strawberry jam	salami
peanut butter	baloney
peanut butter and honey	chicken
cream cheese and jelly	roast beef
jelly without peanut butter	ham
jelly without cream cheese	turkey
American cheese	tuna fish
Swiss cheese	

He had to ask Karen and Elaine to help him spell

some of the words. Then Aldo went into the kitchen where his mother was just finishing straightening up after supper.

"Did you make my lunch for tomorrow yet?" Aldo asked.

"No. I'm just getting ready to do it now," Mrs. Sossi said.

"Here," said Aldo, and he handed his list to his mother.

"What is this?" she asked. "Another list? There are too many lists in this house already."

"I decided that I don't want to eat any more animals," said Aldo. "It's like killing. So just give me the 'yes' sandwiches and none of the 'no' sandwiches."

Mr. Sossi walked into the kitchen and looked at the paper with his wife. "It will be hard to tell the difference between a jelly-without-pea-nut-butter sandwich and a jelly-without-cream-cheese sandwich," he said, after studying the list for a minute.

"Aldo, does this mean that you don't plan to eat any meat at all?" asked his mother.

"Yes," said Aldo. "I've been thinking about how many animals die so people can eat."

"Oh, let him try it for a few days," agreed Mr. Sossi. "It can't hurt him, and besides I know Aldo. He'll never be able to resist when he's offered a hot dog."

"Hot dogs?" said Aldo. He hadn't thought about hot dogs. He knew they weren't made out of dogs, but what type of animal were they?

"This is going to make life very complicated for me," complained Mrs. Sossi. "What will you eat for dinner?"

"He can eat spaghetti without the meatballs," said Mr. Sossi. "I can assure you he won't starve. They say Americans eat too much meat, anyhow. Give him eggs and cheese instead."

"I still think that I ought to check this out with the pediatrician," said Mrs. Sossi uncertainly. "Elaine and Karen never went through a phase like this."

Mrs. Sossi reached for the peanut-butter jar in order to make Aldo's lunch for the next day.

Peabody came into the kitchen, followed by

Poughkeepsie. They both began meowing a complaint.

"Aldo, did you remember to feed the cats?" asked his mother.

Aldo had been so busy writing his sandwich lists that he had forgotten his evening chore. He went to the cupboard and removed a can of cat food. He looked at the label, which said chicken flavor.

"No, Aldo," said Mr. Sossi, reading Aldo's mind. "You can't make the cats become vegetarians just because *you* don't want to eat meat. That is against nature. It's like asking a cow to give up grass."

"I know," said Aldo. Sometimes the cats liked to nibble on a tiny piece of American cheese. But he had to admit to himself that he had never heard of a cat that ate peanut-butter sandwiches, with or without jelly.

9

Chickenless Soup

The first few days after Aldo became a vegetarian were not too hard at all. He had peanut-butter or cheese sandwiches for lunch. At dinner time he ate everything except the meat: spaghetti without meatballs, lots of mashed potatoes when he passed up the chicken. At last he had the perfect excuse not to eat liver, which he had always disliked anyhow. Saturday evening the family went out to a Chinese restaurant. It was hard to pass up the barbecued spare ribs, but Aldo kept reminding himself about the crickets and had vegetable chop suey instead.

Temptation struck on Monday afternoon.

Aldo came home from school famished. His stomach had long forgotten the cream-cheese-and-jelly sandwich that it had consumed at lunchtime. Aldo walked into the house ready to eat almost anything. Mrs. Sossi was busy talking on the telephone. Aldo went into the kitchen, looking for a good snack. He smelled something simmering on the stove. It was the large kettle that his mother used for soup. Little wisps of steam were raising the lid on the pot ever so slightly, and the aroma coming out intrigued Aldo. It smelled a little like chicken soup. His stomach began to make gurgling sounds the way it sometimes did when he was very hungry. His mouth began to salivate. Chicken soup? When was the last time that he had eaten chicken soup? Usually Mrs. Sossi just opened a can of soup, but very occasionally she would make a big pot of soup. Aldo remembered the taste—soft little pieces of chicken, bits of carrots and onions. He had said that he wasn't going to eat chicken anymore, but chicken inside of soup wasn't like eating roast chicken or fried chicken. Then he saw whole pieces of the animal on his plate. If he had roast chicken, he had to watch as the legs and wings were cut off, and the dead animal was chopped to pieces in front of his eyes. Chicken inside of chicken soup was cut up into tiny little bits. It didn't even look like meat at all.

Aldo's stomach made another sound. It was reminding Aldo to stop thinking and to start eating. Aldo went to the cupboard and took out a soup bowl, and then he got himself a soup spoon from the drawer. He wasn't even going to wait until suppertime. He had to have some of the soup now. He wondered if there were noodles in it. Sometimes his mother used noodles, and other times she used rice. Aldo got out a box of crackers. He liked to crumble bits of cracker into his soup.

"I'm sorry, crickets," he whispered to himself. He knew the crickets didn't really care what he ate. And he knew his mother would be pleased if he stopped being a vegetarian. Elaine would tease him, but she would tease him no matter what he did.

Aldo went to the drawer where his mother kept her kitchen utensils and took out the big soup ladle. From the hallway he could hear her still talking on the telephone. It always amazed him how much his mother had to say on the telephone. Sometimes she would talk through two whole television programs.

He took the ladle and went to the pot. It was steaming away, and so even though there was a handle on the pot, which was made of a special, heat-resistant plastic, Aldo decided that he had better get a pot holder. Once more his stomach grumbled. It couldn't understand all these delays. Finally, Aldo lifted the lid from the kettle. He took a deep whiff of the soup as the steam cleared away. He looked into the pot. It was blue! Not the pot, but the soup cooking inside it. Blue soup! Aldo dropped the lid on the floor.

Just then Mrs. Sossi returned to the kitchen. "Aldo, what are you doing?" she asked.

"I wanted some soup," said Aldo. He was about to ask his mother what vegetable made blue soup. Whatever it was he was sure he didn't want any. Even if he was a vegetarian.

His mother laughed. "Aldo," she said, "this is a special plant food that I'm brewing. Mrs. Cohen recommended it to me. If you water your plants with it once every couple of weeks, they thrive better during the winter. I was just warming the mixture a little when the phone rang. Now it has gotten so hot, I'll have to wait for it to cool off."

She looked at the bowl that Aldo had set on the table. "I don't know what this stuff would do to kids. Let's not try it to find out. You're not a plant after all." She laughed again.

"Shall I open a can of chicken-noodle soup for you?" she asked.

"Oh, no," said Aldo. "Don't forget, I'm a vegetarian now."

76

He satisfied his hungry stomach with crackers without any soup. And later, after the liquid in the pot had cooled, Aldo helped his mother water the plants with the chickenless blue soup.

10

Bad News
for the Chameleons

At school, Aldo was disgusted to see that everyone seemed to have forgotten about the crickets
and their fate. Jennifer and Lisa were already
busy thinking up names for the chameleons—
stupid names like Donald Duck and Mickey
Mouse. One they called Clark Kent, because he
would lie quietly in the terrarium and then suddenly jump up and move about climbing over
the grass and the crickets. As far as Aldo could
tell, none of the crickets had been eaten yet.

"It will probably take the chameleons a few
more days to settle down. When they feel com-

pletely at home, they will eat their first meals," explained Mrs. Dowling.

"Yum, yum," said Craig, smacking his lips and pretending to eat a cricket.

Everyone thought he was very funny. Everyone that is except Aldo.

As the week progressed, Aldo continued to study the crickets in the terrariums. Once he couldn't believe his eyes. Bunny and Bugs were actually climbing onto the back of Mickey Mouse. He tapped with his fingernail on the side of the tank to warn them. Didn't they realize that the chameleon that was lying there so quietly might suddenly turn his head and gobble them up like barbecued chickens?

During the morning as his classmates finished their work they went to the back of the room. Everyone wanted to watch how the chameleons changed colors. But even though they were placed on sheets of blue or red construction paper, they didn't change. Then Jessica accidentally dropped one of the chameleons, and he changed from green to gray with fright. If the crickets knew what was going to happen to them, they would change color with fright too, thought Aldo. But the crickets continued to hop about in the terrariums and to chirp happily. They certainly were stupid.

Finally it happened. Bruce and Craig were watching the terrariums and both shouted out at the same time. Donald Duck was stalking a cricket. Everyone rushed to the back of the room, and there were so many people standing about the tank that luckily Aldo couldn't see Donald pounce on a cricket. (It was one of the Seven Dwarf namesakes, but no one was sure which was the actual victim.)

A couple of kids made noises to show their distaste for such a meal, but most of the children cheered Donald on. "Don't you want some ketchup?" asked Peter.

Aldo felt sick. He knew he couldn't bear to remain in class and listen and watch as one by one each of the crickets was sacrificed to satisfy the hunger of the chameleons. He would have to think of something. All during arithmetic and spelling his mind was on the crickets. Even when the class went to the gym, Aldo couldn't keep his mind on the game. It was "Steal the Bacon," which made him think of baby pigs. By the time lunch came, he had made a plan.

Aldo lined up with his classmates when the bell rang. But when he reached the lunchroom, he went to Mrs. Peterson, who was in charge, and told her that he had forgotten his milk money in his desk. She gave him permission to return to his empty classroom. Aldo entered the room and closed the door behind him. He stood quietly for a moment as he rehearsed his plan. His heart was thumping rapidly as he thought about it. He had decided that he would open the terrariums and release all the crickets. Yet, even as he opened the first tank and reached in for George and Martha Washington, he realized the impossibility of his task. In the few weeks that the crickets had been in the classroom, several of the females had laid eggs. Now there were so many baby crickets that it would be impossible to catch them all quickly. Aldo changed his mind. He would remove the chameleons from the tanks instead. The problem now was, what should he do with them after he took them out of the terrariums?

He looked desperately about the room. He saw Mrs. Dowling's desk, and suddenly he remembered how Peabody had hidden in the drawer of Elaine's desk. With two chameleons held gently in his left hand, Aldo quickly opened the bottom drawer of his teacher's desk. He put the little reptiles inside and went to get the others. In a minute all four were hidden in the bottom drawer.

The whole adventure had taken only two or three minutes, but Aldo felt as if he had been in the classroom alone for hours. He rushed back to the lunchroom and automatically opened his lunch box. He didn't have any appetite. His mother had a word for the way his stomach was feeling just now. She called it "queasy." Aldo looked at his sandwich. He wasn't sure which kind it was—either jelly without peanut butter or jelly without cream cheese. He forced himself to act natural and to take a bite. His milk money was still in his desk, so he had to eat his sandwich dry.

11

Much Ado About Aldo

The afternoon began quietly. Surprisingly, no one looked inside the terrariums when they returned from lunch. Anyhow, sometimes the crickets or the chameleons couldn't be seen because they were hiding in the grass. "Camouflage," Mrs. Dowling called it. Maybe when they finally noticed that the chameleons were missing, they would think that the crickets ate them, thought Aldo. He wondered about the chameleons hidden in Mrs. Dowling's drawer. He knew they had enough air. Hadn't Peabody remained hidden for almost twenty-four hours?

So he knew he had a little time to think of what to do with them. He couldn't leave them there. Aldo wondered if the chameleons had any thoughts about the drawer. Maybe they thought they were inside another box being sent to another school.

Mrs. Dowling had a filmstrip that she wanted to show the class. Jimmy and Alex pulled down the window shades to darken the classroom.

"Vanessa, please get the extension cord for the film-strip projector," Mrs. Dowling instructed. "It's in my bottom drawer."

Aldo froze. He was the only one in the class who didn't jump when Vanessa let out a loud scream.

Mrs. Dowling came running. The scream had been so loud that Mrs. Kirk from across the hall came running into the room. And worst luck of all, Mr. Howard, the principal, had been passing by in the hallway, and he came running into the classroom too.

In a second Vanessa was laughing because she

saw what had scared her. Mrs. Dowling and Mrs. Kirk were laughing too, with relief. Only Mr. Howard was angry.

"Who is responsible for this joke?" he asked in a stern voice.

Everyone was silent. Vanessa choked back a giggle.

Aldo blushed bright, bright red. He changed color just as if he were a chameleon. Slowly he raised his hand. "I did it," he said, "but it wasn't for a joke."

"That's very interesting," said Mr. Howard. "You had better come to my office and explain it all to me, young man."

Mr. Howard marched out of the room with Aldo following behind. He looked back and saw Mrs. Dowling putting the chameleons back inside the terrariums. Aldo sighed as he followed Mr. Howard. He felt as if he were a cricket going into a chameleon's cage.

Mr. Howard didn't speak to Aldo for a long time. Instead, he phoned Mrs. Sossi and insisted that she come to school because her son had misbehaved. It was at least half an hour before she arrived, breathless and looking very worried.

"I called you, Mrs. Sossi," Mr. Howard said, "because if we allow youngsters to get away with their little jokes in third grade they will be juvenile delinquents by the time they are in sixth grade."

Mrs. Sossi's eyes filled with tears. "There must be an explanation," she said. "Aldo isn't a troublemaker."

Mr. Howard turned to Aldo. "All right, young man. Tell us why you hid those chameleons in your teacher's desk and nearly gave her a heart attack."

It was hard to know where to begin.

"Donald Duck ate one of the Seven Dwarfs this morning," said Aldo. "It was terrible. Next they'll be eating Bunny and Bugs and George Washington." Aldo's voice cracked, and he began to feel tears in his eyes. He felt like a baby crying in the principal's office, but he didn't

care. He had to tell him how awful this project was. "I love the crickets, and I don't want them to die."

Mrs. Sossi interrupted Aldo. "Mr. Howard, did you know that this boy has become a vegetarian because he can't bear to think of animals being slaughtered?" Considering how often Mrs. Sossi complained at the dinner table, she sounded rather proud of him now.

Gradually the whole story came out. Aldo explained about the project. Mr. Howard looked surprised at first and then sympathetic.

"Mrs. Sossi, this is a fine young man you have here," said Mr. Howard, when the whole story had been told. "If there were more young men like Aldo, the world would be a better place to live in." Then he explained to Aldo, just as Mrs. Dowling had explained to the class, that there is a difference between hunting for food and hunting for pleasure. "If birds and reptiles didn't eat crickets and other insects, the world would be overrun. You must understand that it is all part of nature's plan," said Mr. Howard.

"I don't care about all bugs," explained Aldo. "But once you give an animal a name it becomes your friend, just like my cats Peabody and Poughkeepsie at home."

"You are absolutely right, young man," said Mr. Howard. "I will instruct all my teachers not to permit their students to name crickets in the future. It is no wonder that you became so upset." He paused a minute. "Listen," he said, "this project is almost over. How would you like to take a couple of the crickets home as your personal pets?"

Aldo shook his head. "No, thanks," he said.

"No?" said Mrs. Sossi. "Aldo, all you do is talk about crickets all the time. Why don't you want one?"

"I do want one," explained Aldo. "They are really interesting to watch. But I'm afraid Peabody or Poughkeepsie might try to eat it. Remember how Peabody tries to catch flies in the summer."

"That's true," said Mrs. Sossi. She turned to Mr. Howard to explain. "We have two cats who pounce on anything that moves. It's instinct with them."

Mr. Howard smiled at Aldo. "Young man, you certainly seem to understand animals very well. I wouldn't be surprised if someday you became a veterinarian."

Aldo grinned. "I would like that," he said. He could imagine his name in the telephone book, SOSSI, ALDO, Veterinarian-Vegetarian.

The bell had rung for dismissal while they had been sitting in the office. Mrs. Sossi stood and shook hands with Mr. Howard. "I'm glad this was all straightened out," she said.

"All's well that ends well," said Mr. Howard with a smile. Then he added, "Mrs. Sossi, I have good news for you. The next class unit in science for the third grade is on magnets. I think Aldo will enjoy that. And I can guarantee that no student has ever become emotionally involved with magnets."

"Well, it certainly won't affect his eating habits," agreed Mrs. Sossi, laughing.

"Magnets," said Aldo, as he and his mother walked down the hallway toward his classroom. "That sounds interesting; but it can't be as interesting as crickets."

Mrs. Dowling was in the room straightening up her desk. Aldo went to get his jacket while his mother explained briefly about what had caused his uncharacteristic behavior.

Aldo looked at the terrariums containing both crickets and chameleons. He wondered if the crickets understood about the balance of nature. Maybe while they were chirping to each other mother and father crickets told their baby crickets all about life. Maybe they all knew that in time a bird or a reptile was going to eat them. Maybe they didn't mind. Aldo hoped so. Yet somehow, no matter what Mr. Howard or Mrs. Dowling said about nature, Aldo did mind. Someday, he decided, when he was a veterinarian, he would take care of cats, dogs, guinea pigs, turtles, and even insects. Nothing would be too small for him. Even crickets. He would take care of them then.

"Aldo," called Mrs. Dowling. "Your spelling paper today wasn't perfect, but would you like to have a marshmallow anyhow?"

Aldo knew that Mrs. Dowling was trying to make him feel better. He wasn't hungry, but to be polite he walked up to Mrs. Dowling's desk and tried to smile. He put his hand into the bag extended before him and put the soft piece of white candy into his mouth. Then he quickly extracted it. "What are marshmallows made of?" Aldo asked. "I have to be careful of what I eat now that I'm a vegetarian."

"Oh, it's perfectly safe," said Mrs. Dowling. "The gelatin in them comes from sea-weed."

Reassured, Aldo chewed slowly on the marshmallow. From the back of the room came the chirp of one of the crickets. Neither Aldo nor his mother nor Mrs. Dowling said anything. Then Mrs. Dowling broke the silence.

"Aldo," she said, "I've just decided that this class project has continued long enough. Tomorrow we are going to have a lottery, and the winners may take the chameleons home. And as soon as the weather gets a little warmer, we will take a class trip to the park and release the crickets. Of course, they will still be exposed to the trials of nature," she reminded Aldo, whose expression had completely changed while she had been speaking.

"Oh, Mrs. Dowling, that's wonderful," said Aldo, beaming. Suddenly the queasy feeling that had been in his stomach all morning and afternoon and so many other times recently disappeared. Aldo felt great.

"You must be the best teacher in the whole school," he said. And then he added, "In the whole world!"

Aldo reached out toward the bag of marshmallows on Mrs. Dowling's desk. "Is it OK if I take a couple more?" he asked. "I'm starving."

Johanna Hurwitz spent the first fifteen years of her life in New York City walkups. Born in Manhattan, she grew up in the Bronx and earned a B.A. degree from Queens College. She also has an M.S. in Library Science from Columbia University. Formerly children's librarian with the New York Public Library, she has also worked in a variety of library positions in New York City and Long Island.

Currently Mrs. Hurwitz lives in Great Neck, New York, with her husband, two children, and a cat.

John Wallner was born in St. Louis, Missouri, where he earned a B.F.A. in painting and graphics from Washington University. He also has a M.F.A. in graphics and art history from Pratt Institute in Brooklyn, New York. In addition to illustrating many award-winning children's books, Mr. Wallner has lectured and taught. His honors include exhibition in shows at the Corcoran School of Art in Washington, D.C., and the Society of Illustrators. In 1977 he received the Friends of American Writers Award for Best Juvenile Illustrator.

Mr. Wallner and his wife live in Ossining, New York.